MW00764987

FALCON EDDIE

Babette Douglas

Illustrated by
John Johnson

Productions

Kiss A Me™ Productions, Inc. produces toys and booklets for children with an emphasis on love and learning. For more information on how to purchase a Kiss A Me collectible and plush toy or to receive information on additional Kiss A Me products, write or call:

Kiss a me™ Productions

Kiss A Me Productions, Inc.
90 Garfield Ave.
Sayville, NY 11782
888 - KISSAME
888-547-7263

About the Kiss A Me Teacher Creature Series:
This delightfully illustrated series of inspirational books by
Babette Douglas has won praise from parents and educators alike.
Through her wonderful "teacher creatures" she imparts profound lessons of tolerance
and responsible living with heartwarming insights and a humorous touch.

FALCON EDDIE

Written by Babette Douglas
Illustrated by John Johnson

ISBN 1-89034-321-8
Printed in China

www.kissame.com

To *Theresa M. Santmann,*
Who always soars

FALCON: *The falcon is a hawklike bird often captured and trained to hunt other birds in the sport called falconry. Falcons are often called hawks, but they differ from true hawks in having long pointed wings, fairly long tails, and a different kind of flight. Their wing strokes are rapid,* **and they do not soar.**

Once in a tree, upon a branch, within a nest, lay a small perfect egg of delicate hue, delivered lovingly to the nest by a falcon mother. It was the only egg she had delivered, and she had no plans to deliver another for some time. This was to be her first baby, and she was anxious to see him and begin her task of mothering.

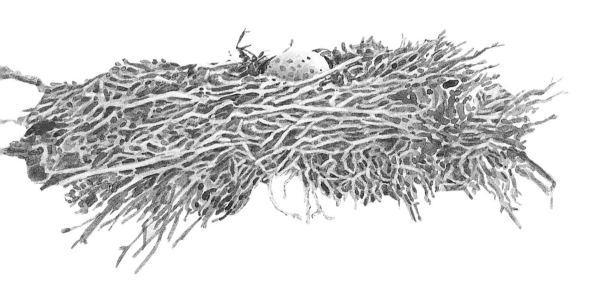

The nest holds a single egg,
Rolling about and free.
No need for a brother or sister,
For mother's the best company.

She warms him when weather is gloomy.
She turns him when cramped he might be.
She names him, "Eddie, my little falcon,"
As she awaits his birth in the tree.

She sits on her egg thus for hours,
With dreams of how great he will be.
Unlike others, he will soar to the mountains,
The greatest of falcons ... and free!

For all of her life she's been tethered,
Tied to some standard or tree.
In dreams she's remained uncaptured.
In dreams she is happy and free.

At last she's becoming a mother
Of a creature she can't wait to see.
With joy she awaits the final moment
When her baby *soars* - high, far and free.

Came the day when at last the egg opened
And there, standing straight as a tree,
Stood the proudest of all baby falcons
Who she knew was born to fly free.

She fed him the best she could give him
Although tethered tight to her tree.
Thus, he proudly kept glowing and growing
As he watched other falcons fly free.

She continued to dream of his soaring,
There upon her high inner view,
Soaring high, high up to the mountains,
Doing what no other falcon could do.

He's ready! And now comes the moment.
With full wings he bursts from the tree.
But instead of soaring, *he settles*,
Afraid at the last to be free.

Mother gently calls out to guide him,
To assure him how great he can be.
But all he remembers beside him
Is his mother tied tight to the tree.

All mothers have wisdom within them.
His distress she could now clearly see.
"He is kept from the air by the vision
Of my long being tied to this tree."

How could she help him to realize
That the strongest prisons we see
Are the ones we make for ourselves
When we decide we can't fly or be free?

She called to her baby to listen
To her words now spoken with care.
"I know you can soar, for I've dreamed it.
Though falcons don't soar, you must dare."

But timid, he jumped from the branches.
He plopped on the ground fast to hide.
The other young falcons just giggled,
"He clearly can't fly or even glide!"

All the young falcons kept flying.
They would dive and swoop through the sky,
But Eddie, the little falcon, kept hiding
And there, while hiding, would cry.

"Everyone now knows I'm frightened.
Although I have wings, I can't fly!
I'll never soar high to the mountains.
In fact, I don't think I will try."

Mother called, "Dearest baby, just listen
To what your heart now begs you to hear.
Never believe for a moment you're helpless.
Never give up hope out of fear.

"If you cannot bear that I'm tethered,
Crying won't wash it away.
Come help as I struggle to freedom
Or here I must continue to stay."

Eddie was left with the challenge,
To hide or to heed what was said.
He decided to help solve the problem
By *not* hiding, but rising instead.

Slowly he climbed a low branch.
Then to the next one he'd climb.
Although he travelled slowly,
As long as he rose, he was fine.

At last at her side, he stood panting.
He held tight to a branch for support.
As he began to help break mother's tether,
All the fears he'd been thinking he thought.

But mother, working quietly, was waiting
For the tether to fall on that day.
Then swift like a falcon she darted
From the tree, like a shot and *away!*

Now Eddie, amazed by her action,
Understood in a flash her display.
She was choosing to rise to her freedom,
Not keep it, by fear, held at bay.

At that moment he realized the great gift
Given him by the mother he adored,
And in a flash he too was flighted.
He lifted - and joyous - he **soared!**

Now...

We must consider each other in living
For our actions affect others each day.
We must pass courage on to our children
For its absence keeps their joy at bay.

To do other in life is deceptive
And teaches our children the lie
That life holds only constraints,
When in truth - given wings - they can fly!

THE END

Babette Douglas, a talented poet and artist, has written over 30 children's books in which diverse creatures live together in harmony, friendship and respect. She brings to her delightful stories the insights and caring accumulated in a lifetime of varied experiences.

"I believe strongly in the healing power of love," she says. "I want to empower children to see with their hearts and to love all the creatures of the earth, including themselves." The unique stories told by her "teacher creatures" enable children to learn to recognize their own gifts and to value tolerance, compassion, optimism and perseverance.

Ms. Douglas, who was born and educated in New York City, has lived in Sayville, New York for over forty years.

Additional Kiss A Me™ *teacher-creature stories:*

AMAZING GRACE

BLUE WISE

BLUFFALO Wins His Great Race

CURLY HARE

THE FLUTTERBY

KISS A ME: A Little Whale Watching

KISS A ME Goes to School

KISS A ME To the Rescue

LARKSPUR

THE LYON BEAR™

THE LYON BEAR™ deTails

THE LYON BEAR™: The Mane Event

MISS EVONNE And the Mice of Nice

MISS TEAK And the Endorphins

NOREEN: The Real King of the Jungle

OSCARPUS

ROSEBUD

SQUIRT: The Magic Cuddle Fish

**Character toys are available for each book.
For additional information on books, toys,
and other products visit us at:**

www.kissame.com